FROSTY the snowman
was a jolly happy soul,
with a corncob pipe and a button nose,
and two eyes made out of coal.

Frosty the snowman, is a fairy tale, they say.
He was made of snow,
but the children know
how he came to life one day.

There must have been some magic in that old silk hat they found.

For when they placed it on his head,
he began to dance around.

Oh, Frosty the snowman
was alive as he could be.
And the children say
he could laugh and play,
just the same as you and me.

Thumpety thump thump,
Thumpety thump thump,
look at Frosty go.

Thumpety thump thump,
Thumpety thump thump,
over the hills of snow.

Frosty the snowman
knew the sun was hot that day.
So he said, "Let's run
and we'll have some fun
now before I melt away."

Down to the village,
with a broomstick in his hand,
running here and there,
all around the square,
saying, "Catch me if you can."

He led them down the streets of town
right to the traffic cop.
And he only paused a moment when
he heard him holler, "Stop!"

Oh, Frosty the snowman
had to hurry on his way.
But he waved good-bye
saying, "Don't you cry,
I'll be back again some day."

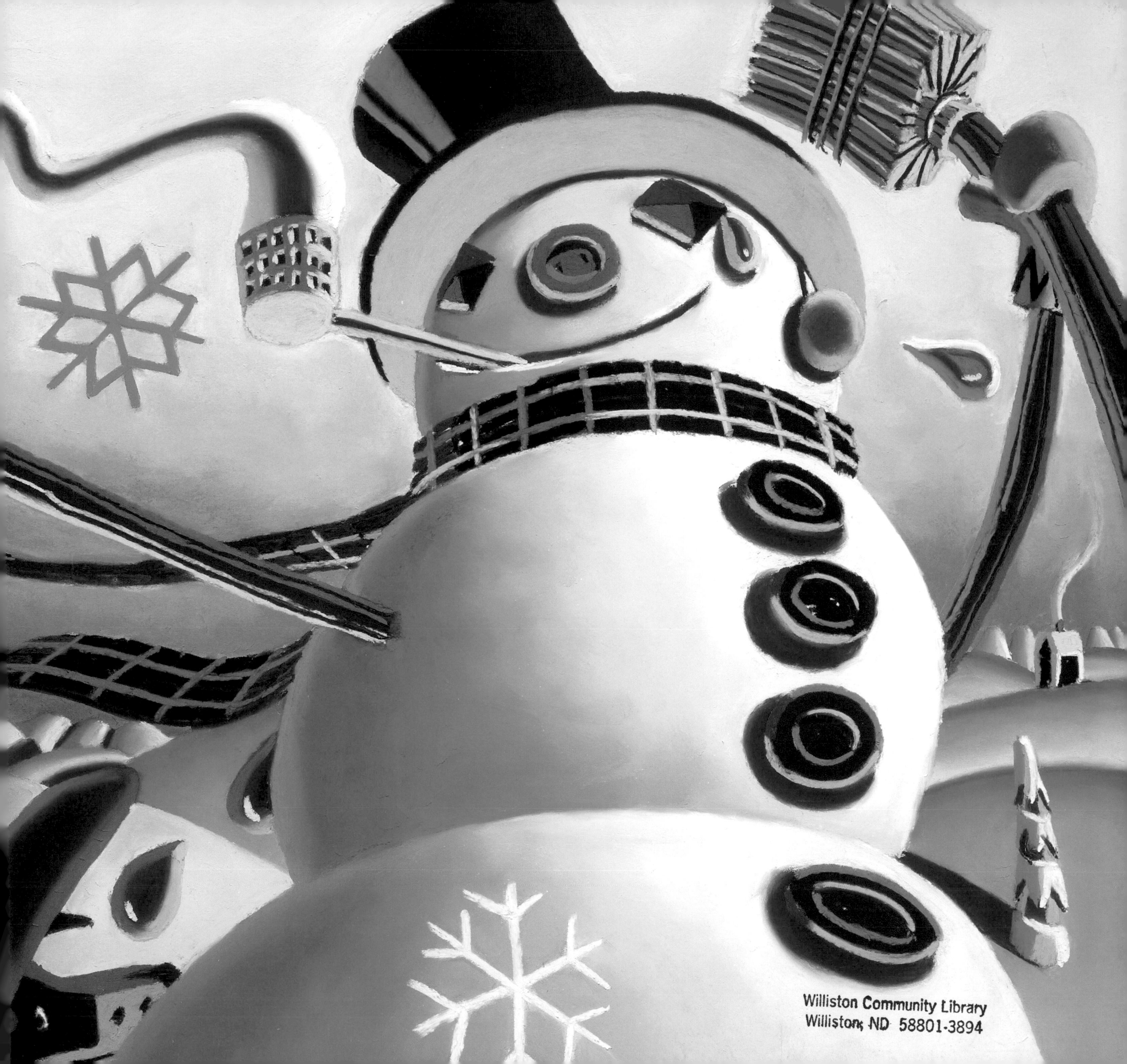

Thumpety thump thump,
Thumpety thump thump,
look at Frosty go.

Thumpety thump thump,
Thumpety thump thump,
over the hills of snow.

Performer's Note

My earliest recollection of "Frosty the Snowman" is as a child in Seattle, Washington, probably around 1952. My dad had a big, beautiful radio and its music would leave me frozen in place whenever I stood near it. December in Seattle was very special for kids, because when it snowed the city would close the roads so that kids could all go sledding in the streets. Our big family outing of the season was to go downtown to Frederick & Nelson department store to see the animatronics elves and reindeer and, of course, Santa, in the store's elaborate holiday windows. It was like a fantasy North Pole come to life as the strains of "Frosty the Snowman," sung by Gene "The Singin' Cowboy" Autry, played softly over the oudoor speakers.

I am honored to put my own spin on such a beloved holiday classic, and sincerely hope you enjoy this beautiful book with your children or grandchildren, as indeed I will with my own for years to come.

Artist's Note

For many years, I have dreamed of illustrating "Frosty the Snowman." In New England, where I live and grew up, there is endless inspiration for this timeless story. In creating the illustrations in this book, I drew upon memories of gray November skies; anticipation of the first snowflake; sketching throughout the day; building snow tunnels, caves, and wall windows until the snow and my fingers turned blue; and putting the finishing touches on my own frosty guardian who would keep us safe through the long winter's night.

Library of Congress Cataloging-in-Publication Data

Nelson, Steve, 1907-1981.
Frosty the snowman / music and lyrics by Steve Nelson and Jack Rollins ;
performed by Kenny Loggins ; illustrated by Wade Zahares.
p. cm.
"An Imagine Book."
Summary: An illustrated version of the song in which a snowman
comes to life and plays with the children who built him.
ISBN 978-1-62354-012-8
1. Children's songs, English—United States—Texts. 2. Snowmen—Songs and
music—Juvenile literature. [1. Songs. 2. Snowmen—Songs and music.] I.
Rollins, Jack, 1906-1973. II. Loggins, Kenny. III. Zahares, Wade, ill. IV.
Title.
PZ8.3.N3645Fr 2013
782.42--dc23
2012046363

3 5 7 9 10 8 6 4 2

An Imagine Book
Published by Charlesbridge
85 Main Street
Watertown, MA 02472
617-926-0329
www.charlesbridge.com

Performed by Kenny Loggins
Illustrated by Wade Zahares